Somewhere not so far away is the Land o
Roo, where Polkaroo lives with his friends
Humpty, Dumpty, Marigold and Bear, an
his pet, Bibble.

One day, Dumpty had a big problem. He decided to write to his friend Polkaroo for some advice.

MW01713797

Dear Polkaroo,

I just don't know what to do! Humpty asked me to wash his favourite blanket – and I wanted to do a really good job, so I washed and washed and washed it. But when I took it out of the dryer, it was *so* small! I didn't know it would shrink!

Humpty will be so upset. He needs his favourite blanket to go to sleep. I even tried stretching Humpty's blanket, but it didn't work!

What am I going to do, Polkaroo? Please help.

Your friend,
Dumpty

P.S. I'm sending this note with Bibble so that I'm here when Humpty comes home for his nap. He will want his clean blanket for nap time.

Dear Polkaroo,
I just don't know what to
do! Humpty asked me to
wash his blanket —
and I wanted to
do a good job. So I
washed and
washed

Dear Dumpty,

I am so sorry to hear about Humpty's blanket. I know how much it meant to him. I hope you did not hurt yourself trying to stretch it! Take some deep breaths and try not to worry.

We'll just have to try and find something else to help Humpty go to sleep. Try giving him this soft, squeaky, polka dot pig to cuddle. I'm sending it over with Bibble. I bet he'll love it.

Your friend,

Polkaroo

Dear Polkaroo,

Thank you for your help. I tried to give Humpty the soft, squeaky, polka dot pig, but he didn't want it. He wants his blanket!

He says that he needs it right now because it is almost nap time.

There is just not another blanket anywhere like his favourite blanket with the "H" for Humpty. How will he ever get to sleep?

Any other ideas, Polkaroo? He's getting very impatient!

Your friend,

Dumpty

Dear Dumpty,

It sounds like Humpty is really missing his special blanket. I hope that Bibble thinks the blanket I'm knitting for him is that great.

Too bad Humpty didn't want the soft, squeaky, polka dot pig. Please don't be too upset. Try giving him these warm, cozy pyjamas. They feel just like his blanket. I'm sure he'll love them!

You can also give him a glass of warm milk before he goes to bed. Maybe that will make him sleepy.

Good luck!

Your friend,

Polkaroo

from
Dumpty

ar Dumpty,
It sounds like Humpty is really missing his
Too bad Humpty didn't want the soft,
squeaky polka dot pig. Please don't be too
upset. Try giving him these warm, cozy pyjamas.
Good luck!
Your friend,
Polkaroo

Dear Polkaroo,

Thanks for sending the warm, cozy pyjamas. However, I'm afraid they didn't quite fit Humpty. He just isn't the same shape you are! Struggling with the pyjamas has made him even more upset. He didn't even want to try the warm milk. All he wants is his blanket.

What am I going to do, Polkaroo? Humpty's *really* tired. Do you think it would help him get to sleep if I just told him what happened and gave him his blanket – even though it's so small?

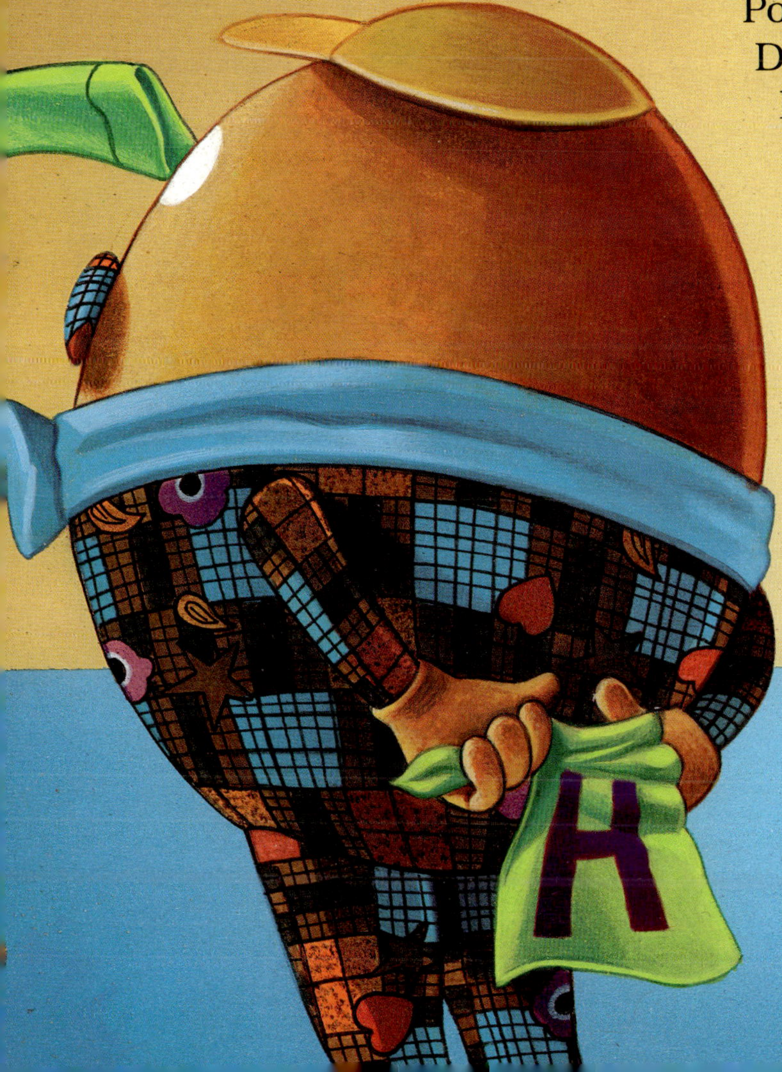

Your friend,

Dumpty

P.S. I'm sure Bibble will love the blanket you're knitting for him.

Dear Polkaroo,
Thanks for
sending the
warm, cozy
pyjamas.
However, I'm
afraid they
didn't
from
Dumpty

Dear Dumpty,

I'm sorry that the cozy pyjamas and warm milk did not help. I guess I am a little taller and thinner than Humpty. I think you should tell Humpty what happened. After all, you were just trying to do your best when you washed his blanket for him.

Your friend,

Polkaroo

P.S. Surprise! I'm sending you the blanket that I started to knit for Bibble. I decided to make it big enough for Humpty when nothing else seemed to help him get to sleep.

I hope he likes it as much as the blanket that shrank.

from Polkaroo

Dear Polkaroo,

What a great friend you are! Thank you for your surprise package. I told Humpty what happened to his blanket. He was upset at first. But when he saw the soft, cozy blanket you knit for him – that even has an 'H' – he was so excited!

And guess what happened when we opened up the blanket? A great big pair of polka dot shorts fell out! How did *they* get there?

Thanks a bunch, Polkaroo!

Your friend,

Dumpty

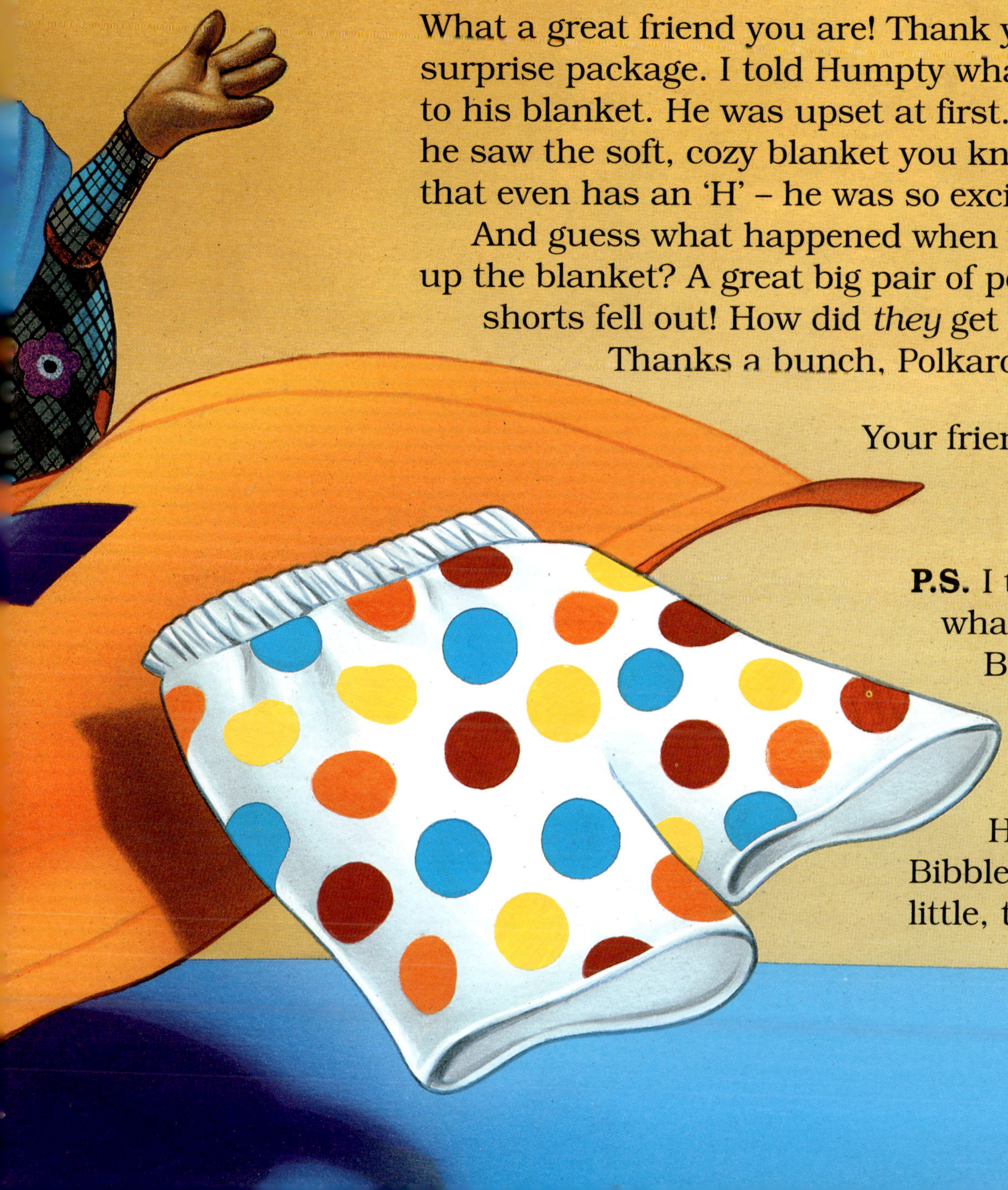

P.S. I told Humpty what a big help Bibble was, taking our letters back and forth. He would like Bibble to have his little, tiny blanket.

You know what, Polkaroo?
I think it's just the right size!